For Mom

with Love

For Mom

A Book of Quotations

Edited by
Mary Carnahan

with Love

Ariel Books

•

**Andrews McMeel
Publishing**

Kansas City

ISBN: 0-7407-1472-4

Library of Congress Catalog Card Number: 00-106941

Contents

Introduction

*Life is the first gift, love is the second,
and understanding the third.*

MARGE PIERCY

The radiant, unconditional love of a
mother's gaze, the warmth and comfort of
her arms—encompassing and permeating our
childhoods, she is the center of our tiny universe,

our compass. Always at our side, kissing the hurts, urging us over and around the hurdles, she cheers us on, always on our team.

A mother's love and dreams guide us like an invisible star, and we shape our own lives and families as variations on patterns handed down over the generations. Sometimes pleased, sometimes shocked, we become our parents as we become ourselves. We change, and the world changes around us; still, as children, young adults, and parents, mother is the map we use to chart ourselves. And as we grow, we find the gifts of patience, strength, common sense, and wisdom left in our minds and hearts, a loving time capsule planted when we weren't looking.

This book celebrates mothers and the invisible bond that holds us to them all our lives.

Early & Years

*Y*our children are not your children. They are the sons and daughters of life's longing for itself. They come through you but not from you, and though they are with you, yet they belong not to you.

Kahlil Gibran

*I*n the sheltered simplicity of the first days after a baby is born, one sees again the magical closed circle, the miraculous sense of two people existing only for each other.

Anne Morrow Lindbergh

*M*y child looked at me and I looked back at him in the delivery room, and I realized that out of a sea of infinite possibilities it had come down to this: a specific person, born on the hottest day of the year, conceived on a Christmas Eve, made by his father and me miraculously from scratch.

Anna Quindlen

Maternal love, like an orange tree, buds and blossoms and bears at once. When a woman puts her finger for the first time into the tiny hand of her baby and feels that helpless clutch which tightens her very heartstrings, she is born again with the newborn child.

Kate Douglas Wiggin

When you are a mother, you are never really alone in your thoughts. You are connected to your child and to all those who touch your lives. A mother always has to think twice, once for herself and once for her child.

Sophia Loren

I looked at this tiny, perfect creature and it was as though a light switch had been turned on. A great rush of love, mother love, flooded out of me.

Madeleine L'Engle

*I*s not a young mother one of the
sweetest sights life shows us?

William Makepeace Thackeray

$\mathcal{W}$omen know the way to rear up
   children. . . .
They know a simple, merry, tender knack
Of tying sashes, fitting baby-shoes,
And stringing pretty words that make no
   sense. . . .

Elizabeth Barrett Browning

*T*he walks and talks we have with our two-year-olds in red boots have a great deal to do with the values they will cherish as adults.

Edith F. Hunter

*E*ducation is the mental railway, beginning at birth and running on to eternity. No hand can lay it in the right direction but the hand of a mother.

Mrs. H. O. Ward

$\mathcal{T}$he mother should teach her
daughter above all things to know herself.

C. E. Sargent

*I*t's the little things you do
day in and day out that count. That's the way
you teach your children.

Amanda Pays

They always looked back before turning the corner, for their mother was always at the window to nod and smile, and wave her hand at them. Somehow it seemed as if they couldn't have got through the day without that, for whatever their mood might be, the last glimpse of that motherly face was sure to affect them like sunshine.

Louisa May Alcott

*I*n a child's
lunch basket, a
mother's thoughts.

Japanese proverb

The child, in the decisive first years of his life, has the experience of his mother, as an all-enveloping, protective, nourishing power. Mother is food; she is love; she is warmth; she is earth. To be loved by her means to be alive, to be rooted, to be at home.

Erich Fromm

I was not a classic mother. But my kids were never palmed off to boarding school. So I didn't bake cookies. You can buy cookies, but you can't buy love.

Raquel Welch

*Y*our children need your
presence more than they need your presents.

Jesse Jackson

The goodness of a home is
not dependent on wealth, or spaciousness, or
beauty, or luxury. Everything depends on the
Mother.

G. W. Russell

*E*very person needs recognition. It is expressed cogently by the child who says, "Mother, let's play darts. I'll throw the darts and you say, 'wonderful.'"

M . Dale Baugham

*M*otherhood is *not* for the
fainthearted. Used frogs, skinned knees,
and the insults of teenage girls are not
meant for the wimpy.

Danielle Steele

*N*obody said giving birth
is easy, but there's no other way to get the
job done.

Ivana Trump

A suburban mother's role
is to deliver children obstetrically once, and
by car for ever after.

Peter De Vries

*I*t goes without saying, you should never have more children than you have car windows.

Erma Bombeck

*I*t seems to me I spent my life
in car pools, but you know, that's how I kept
track of what was going on.

Barbara Bush

*A*ny mother could perform
the jobs of several air-traffic controllers
with ease.

Lisa Alther

*N*obody knows of the work it
   makes
To keep the home together,
Nobody knows of the steps it takes,
Nobody knows—but mother.

Anonymous

I figure if the kids are alive
at the end of the day, I've done my job.

Roseanne

*T*here never was a child so
lovely but his mother was glad to get
him asleep.

Ralph Waldo Emerson

*H*aving children is like
having a bowling alley installed in your brain.

Martin Mull

There are so many disciplines in being a parent besides the obvious ones like getting up in the night and putting up with the noise during the day. And almost the hardest of all is learning to be a well of affection and not a fountain, to show them we love them, not when *we* feel like it, but when they do.

Nan Fairbrother

[*P*arents] must get across
the idea that "I love you always, but sometimes I do not love your behavior."

Amy Vanderbilt

*B*e your
children's best
teacher and coach.

Life's Little Instruction
Book, Vol. II

The thing that impresses me most about America is the way parents obey their children.

King Edward VIII (Duke of Windsor)

*T*he real menace in dealing
with a five-year-old is that in no time at all
you begin to sound like a five-year-old.

Jean Kerr

$\mathcal{R}$easoning with a child is
fine, if you can reach the child's reason
without destroying your own.

John Mason Brown

*I*nsanity is hereditary—
you get it from your kids.

Sam Levinson

Children are a great comfort
in your old age—and they help you to reach
it faster too.

Lionel M. Kauffman

The two things children
wear out are clothes and parents.

Anonymous

*I*f there were no schools to take the children away from home part of the time, the insane asylum would be filled with mothers.

Edgar Watson Howe

*S*urrendering to motherhood
means surrendering to interruption.

Erica Jong

$\mathcal{P}$arenthood: that state of
being better chaperoned than you were
before marriage.

Marceline Cox

*M*ore than in any other
human relationship, overwhelmingly
more, motherhood means being instantly
interruptible, responsive, responsible.

Tillie Olsen

$\mathcal{T}$he quickest way for a parent
to get a child's attention is to sit down and
look comfortable.

Lane Olinhouse

$\mathcal{T}$he most effective form of
birth control I know is spending the day
with my kids.

Jill Bensley

When my kids become
wild and unruly, I use a nice, safe playpen.
When they're finished, I climb out.

Erma Bombeck

*C*leaning your house while
your kids are still growing is like shoveling
the walk before it stops snowing.

Phyllis Diller

$\mathcal{M}$y mother had a great deal of trouble with me, but I think she enjoyed it.

Mark Twain

When I was six I made my mother a little hat—out of her new blouse.

Lilly Dache

*P*ersonally, Veda's convinced
me that alligators have the right idea. They
eat their young.

Eve Arden
in Mildred Pierce

$\mathcal{A}$ woman who can cope
with the terrible twos can cope with
anything.

Judith Clabes

*N*ow, as always, the most automated appliance in a household is the mother.

Beverley Jones

*Y*ou become about as exciting
as your food blender. The kids come in, look
you in the eye, and ask if anybody's home.

Erma Bombeck

*C*hildren aren't happy with nothing to
   ignore,
And that's what parents were created for.

Ogden Nash

*W*e never know the love
of our parents for us till we have become
parents.

Henry Ward Beecher

$\mathcal{T}$here are times when
parenthood seems nothing more than feeding
the hand that bites you.

Peter De Vries

*M*others have to handle all kinds of situations. When presented with the new baby brother he said he wanted, the toddler told his mother, "I changed my mind."

Judith Viorst

Most mothers are instinctive philosophers.

Harriet Beecher Stowe

A mother understands
what a child does not say.

Yiddish proverb

*M*other is the name for
God in the lips and hearts of children.

William Makepeace
Thackeray

She is their earth. . . . She is their food and their bed and the extra blanket when it grows cold in the night; she is their warmth and their health and their shelter.

Katherine Butler Hathaway

*L*oving a child doesn't mean giving in to all his whims; to love him is to bring out the best in him, to teach him to love what is difficult.

Nadia Boulanger

As a parent you try to maintain a certain amount of control and so you have this tug-of-war. . . . You have to learn when to let go. And that's not easy.

Aretha Franklin

Do not, on a rainy day, ask your child what he feels like doing, because I assure you that what he feels like doing, you won't feel like watching.

Fran Lebowitz

*A*t night, when the house is quiet and the children have all gone to sleep, I take a deep breath and listen to the steady beat of my heart.

Jillian Klarl

*D*oes it seem impossible that the child will grow up? That the bashful smile will become a bold expression . . . that a briefcase will replace the blue security blanket?

Anne Beattie

$\mathcal{H}$old your child's hand
every chance you get. The time will come all
too soon when he or she won't let you.

Life's Little Instruction
Book, Vol. II

$\mathcal{F}$rom the time she was born, until
she was fifteen, I didn't know where I left
off and she began. We were joined at the
hip or the heart or the brain.

Lee Grant

$\mathcal{I}$t will be gone before you know it. The fingerprints on the wall appear higher and higher. Then suddenly they disappear.

Dorothy Evslin

We had a disappointing experience with our children—they all grew up.

Leslie Bonaventure

Throughout
Life

*Y*our children are always
your "babies," even if they have gray hair.

Janet Leigh

*T*he older I become,
the more I think about my mother.

Ingmar Bergman

*Y*ou never get over being
a child, long as you have a mother to go to.

Sarah Orne Jewett

Mothers never change, I guess,
In their tender thoughtfulness.
All her gentle long life through
She is bent on nursing you;
An' although you may be grown,
She still claims you for her own,
An' to her you'll always be
Just a youngster at her knee.

Edgar A. Guest

*A*s you grow older, the years
in between seem to get smaller and smaller.
It's not like a parent and a child anymore.
The gap closes, and it becomes a friendship.

Julianne Phillips

There is a point where you aren't
as much mom and daughter as you are
adults and friends. It doesn't happen for
everyone—but it did for Mom and me.

Jamie Lee Curtis

Who is getting more pleasure
from this rocking, the baby or me?

Nancy Thayer

A mother is the truest friend we have when trials, heavy and sudden, fall upon us; when adversity takes the place of prosperity.

Washington Irving

We are together, my child
and I, Mother and child, yes, but *sisters* really,
against whatever denies us all that we are.

Alice Walker

*W*hat *do* girls do who haven't any mothers to help them through their troubles?

Louisa May Alcott

There is in all this cold and hollow
   world
No fount of deep, strong, deathless love;
Save that within a mother's heart.

Felicia Hemans

*W*hat do we mean by the nurture of daughters? What is it we wish we had, or could have, as daughters; could give, as mothers? Deeply and primally we need trust and tenderness; surely this will always be true of every human being, but women growing into a world so hostile to us need a very profound kind of loving in order to learn to love ourselves.

Adrienne Rich

*T*oday's mothers have certain
values, hard-won, in common. Primary is
the conviction that their daughters must be
defined from the inside out as opposed to
the reverse.

Phyllis Theroux

*I*n passing we may say that a girl is always safe who gives a wise and loving mother her entire confidence, and a mother is her child's very best counselor and chaperone.

Margaret E. Sangster

$\mathcal{G}$od intended motherhood to
be a relay race. Each generation would pass
the baton on to the next.

Mary Pride

The debt of gratitude we owe our mother and father goes forward, not backward. What we owe our parents is the bill presented to us by our children.

Nancy Friday

*M*others of daughters are
daughters of mothers and have remained so,
in circles joined to circles, since time began.

Signe Hammer

*O*ur mothers are our most
direct connection to our history and
our gender.

Hope Edelman

The first time I realized I had become my mother was when I moved into my new apartment. It has this amazing, fully equipped kitchen—and I ordered in Chinese food. I'm the worst cook ever— just like my mother.

Ricki Lake

*M*y mother won't admit it, but I've always been a disappointment to her. Deep down inside, she'll never forgive herself for giving birth to a daughter who refuses to launder aluminum foil and use it over again.

Erma Bombeck

$\mathcal{M}$aybe Mom is my alter
ego and the woman I'm able to be when I'm
working.

M a r y   T y l e r   M o o r e

From the time I was a child I wanted to be like my mother. Not necessarily an actress—I never dreamed I'd have the courage—but an active, volatile woman like she was.

Isabella Rossellini

The relationship between a mother and her daughter is as varied, as mysterious, as constantly changing and interconnected as the patterns that touch, move away from, and touch again in a kaleidoscope.

Lyn Lifshin

$\mathcal{T}$here is an important line
between mother and daughter, mother and
friend.

Phyllis Magrab

She told me she thinks I'm a son of a bitch. She also thinks I'm a funny son of a bitch. She loves me, but she doesn't like me. She's afraid of me, she's intimidated by me. She respects me, but she doesn't want to become like me. We have a perfectly normal mother–daughter relationship.

Jane Fonda
in California Suite

A daughter looking at her mother's life is looking at her own, shaping and fitting one life to suit the needs of another. Some have shaped monsters and some angels. Most who make angels see their mother as the sources of art, the tree of creative life.

Louise Bernikow

$\mathcal{F}$ifty-four years of love and tenderness
and crossness and devotion and unswerving
loyalty. Without her I could have achieved a
quarter of what I have achieved, not only in
terms of success and career, but in terms of
personal happiness. . . . She has never stood
between me and my life, never tried to hold
me too tightly, always let me go free.

Noel Coward

*J*ust as the ripe fruit breaks off from the tree, so a time will come when you will have to break off from your mother. It's sad—sad for me too. But it's something to be glad about for your sake, since it means that you are growing up.

Isoko Hatano

$\mathcal{T}$he amicable loosening of
the bond between daughter and mother is
one of the most difficult tasks of education.

Alice Balint

The mother-child relationship is paradoxical and, in a sense, tragic. It requires that most intense love on the mother's side, yet this very love must help the child grow away from the mother and become fully independent.

Erich Fromm

I couldn't have a better friend than my mother. I never had to be afraid to talk to her about anything. . . . And the basic things that my mother taught me are pretty much right on. But she never restricted. . . . If I wanted to do something that she didn't approve of she'd say, "Well, I usually tell you how it is. If you want to go ahead and do this, it's up to you. But just know that I don't approve."

Lacy J. Dalton

*W*here do mothers learn all
the things they tell their daughters not to do?

Evan Esar

What the daughter does, the mother did.

Jewish proverb

A mother's example
sketches the outline of her child's character.

Mrs. H. O. Ward

*B*ut what mother and daughter understand each other, or even have the sympathy for each other's lack of understanding?

Maya Angelou

My mother had a problem
because she grew up during the Great
Depression. And I had problems because
I grew up during her great depression.

Jane Stroll

Whenever I'm with my mother, I feel as though I have to spend the whole time avoiding land mines.

Amy Tan

*N*o matter how perfect
your mother thinks you are, she will always
want to fix your hair.

Suzanne Beilenson

There are many things I will never forgive my mother for, but heading the list is the fact that she did the Double-Crostic in ink.

Nora Ephron

*M*y mother phones daily to ask, "Did you just try to reach me?" When I reply, "No," she adds, "So, if you're not too busy, call me while I'm still alive," and hangs up.

Erma Bombeck

*A*cknowledging the tension, distance, and conflict, where is a map of the nurturance, the connection, the ways in which the torch is passed from mother to daughter or from daughter to mother?

Colette

$\mathcal{I}$f you have never been hated
by your child, you have never been a
parent.

Bette Davis

$\mathcal{Y}$our mother's always wrong;
that's why they made her your mother.

Bruce Jay Friedman

*L*ike all parents who reach a
point of total frustration with the adolescent
animal, my mother had taunted that she
wished she could be a fly on the wall to see
how I handled having a family.

Quo Vadis Gex-Breaux

When we weren't scratching each other's eyes out, we were making each other laugh harder than anyone else could.

Lucie Arnaz,
on her mother, Lucille Ball

*C*hildren
are what the
mothers are.

Walter Savage Landor

The daughter begins to bloom before the mother can be content to fade, and neither can forbear to wish for the absence of the other.

Samuel Johnson

*I*t's agony and ecstasy. There's no question that the mother-daughter relationship is the most complex on earth. It's even more complicated than the man–woman thing.

Naomi Judd

I spent hours rummaging through my mother's drawers, dabbing her cologne behind my ears, putting on her rhinestone earrings, reading anniversary cards my father had given her, sifting through the hodgepodge in her pocketbooks. I was hunting for clues about what it was to be a woman. I was searching for some secret I knew she had, but wouldn't willingly share with me.

Angela Barron McBride

*A*nd maybe it's time we admitted that a lot of the traits—good and bad—we blame on Mom would be better attributed to life.

Sara Nelson

*I*t is very difficult to live
among people you love and hold back from
offering them advice.

Anne Tyler

Adolescence is a twentieth-century invention most parents approach with dread and look back on with the relief of survivors.

Faye Moskowitz

With any child entering adolescence,
one hunts for signs of health, is desperate
for the smallest indication that the child's
problems will never be important enough
for a television movie.

Delia Ephron

*M*y mother was an authority on pigsties. "This is the worst-looking pigsty I have ever seen in my life, and I want it cleaned up right now."

Bill Cosby

$\mathcal{M}$isery is when you make
your bed and then your mother tells you it's
the day she's changing the sheets.

Suzanne   Heller

*I*f one is not going to take the necessary precautions to avoid having parents, one must undertake to bring them up.

Quentin Crisp

The essential thing about mothers—
one needs to know that they are there,
particularly at that age when, paradoxically,
one is trying so hard to break away from
parental influence.

Margot Fonteyn

A mother's love is the golden link
Binding youth to age;
And he is still but a child,
However time may have furrowed his
    cheek,
Who cannot happily recall, with a soft-
    ened heart,
The fond devotion and gentle chidings
Of the best friend God ever gave.

Christian Bovée

*B*efore becoming a mother I had a hundred theories on how to bring up children. Now I have seven children and only one theory: Love them, especially when they least deserve to be loved.

Kate Samperi

I think my life began with
waking up and loving my mother's face.

George Eliot

The source
of human love is
the mother.

African proverb

*O*n the plane flying home [from visiting Grandma], with Audrey in my arms, I thought about mothers and daughters, and the four generations of the family that I know most intimately. Every one of those mothers loves and needs her daughter more than her daughter will love or need her some day, and we are, each of us, the only person on earth who is quite so consumingly interested in our child.

Joyce Maynard

 $\mathcal{M}$ other love is so powerful
and primitive that it feels . . . "like the doctor
forgot to cut the umbilical cord."

Anonymous

*L*oving a child is a circular
business. . . . The more you give, the more
you get, the more you get, the more you
want to give.

Penelope Leach

*M*otherhood has been the
most joyous and important experience of my
life. I would die for my children.

Carly Simon

*T*o a mother, children are
   like ideas;
none are as wonderful as her own.

Chinese saying

*I*n the eyes of
its mother every
beetle is a gazelle.

Moroccan proverb

$\mathcal{R}$omance fails us and so do friendships, but the relationship of parent and child, less noisy than all others, remains indelible and indestructible, the strongest relationship on earth.

Theodor Reik

$\mathcal{A}$ man loves his sweetheart the most, his wife the best, but his mother the longest.

Irish proverb

$\mathcal{D}$on't aim to be an earthly Saint,
    with eyes fixed on a star,
Just try to be the fellow that your Mother
    thinks you are.

Will Sadkin

There is nothing so strong as the force of love; there is no love so forcible as the love of an affectionate mother to her natural child.

Elizabeth Grymeston

To love the tender heart hath ever
fled,
As on its mother's breast the infant throws
Its sobbing face, and there in sleep forgets
its woe.

Mary Tighe

*M*other—that was the
bank where we deposited all our hurts
and worries.

T. Dewitt Talmage

*W*ho ran to help me when I fell,
And would some pretty story tell,
Or kiss the place to make it well?
My Mother.

Ann Taylor

$\mathcal{T}$he heart of a mother is a
deep abyss at the bottom of which you will
always discover forgiveness.

Honoré de Balzac

*S*ome are kissing mothers and some
are scolding mothers, but it is love just the
same, and most mothers kiss and scold
together.

Pearl S. Buck

I have found that no kisses can ever compare to "mom" kisses, because mom kisses can heal anything. You can have a hangnail, a broken heart, or catatonic schizophrenia; with moms, one kiss and you're fine.

Robert G. Lee

There is no influence so
powerful as that of the mother.

Sarah Josepha Hale

My mother's hands are cool and
    fair,
They can do anything.
Delicate mercies hide them there
Like flowers in the spring.

Anna Hempstead Branch

*P*robably there is nothing in human nature more resonant with charges than the flow of energy between two biologically alike bodies, one of which has lain in amniotic bliss inside the other, one of which has labored to give birth to the other. The materials are here for the deepest mutuality and the most painful estrangement.

Adrienne Rich

$\mathcal{M}$y sister said once:
"Anything I don't want Mother to know,
I don't even *think* of, if she's in the room."

Agatha Christie

Mother love makes a
woman more vulnerable than any other
creature on earth.

Pam Brown

We are transfused into our children and . . . feel more keenly for them than for ourselves.

Marie de Sévigné

She weeps for him a mother's burning tears—
She loved him with a mother's deepest
   love.

Paul Laurence Dunbar

I have heard daughters say that they do not love their mothers. I have *never* heard a mother say she does not love her daughter.

Nancy Friday

I got more children than I
can rightly take care of, but I ain't got more
than I can love.

Ossie Guffy

*W*e are all daughters of the present,
with the potential to impact a new motherhood as well as a new womanhood. But
regardless of the changes that occur . . .
there always will be a unique tie between
mother and daughter in our society.

Phyllis Magrab

$\mathcal{A}$nd it came to me, and I knew what I had to have before my soul would rest. I wanted to belong—to belong to my mother. And in return—I wanted my mother to belong to me.

Gloria Vanderbilt

*S*he was such a good loving mother, my best friend; oh, who was happier than I when I could still say the dear name "mother," and it was heard, and whom can I say it to now?

Ludwig van Beethoven

*N*ow in memory comes my mother,
As she used, in years agone,
To regard the darling dreamers
Ere she left them till the dawn.

Coates Kinney

*A*ll the earth, though it were full of kind hearts, is but a desolation and a desert place to a mother when her only child is absent.

Elizabeth Gaskell

*S*he never outgrows the
burden of love, and to the end she carries the
weight of hope for those she bore.

Florida Scott-Maxwell

You have to love your children unselfishly. That's hard. But it's the only way.

Barbara Bush

*I*n a Chinese family the mother pulls very tightly on the bond to a point where the daughter asks, "Why can't I know about such and such?" and the mother answers, "Because I haven't put it into your mind yet."

Amy Tan

*A*ll mothers are rich when they love their children. There are no poor mothers, no ugly ones, no old ones. Their love is always the most beautiful of joys.

Maurice Maeterlinck

*T*o my mother I tell the truth. I have no thought, no feeling that I cannot share with my mother, and she is like a second conscience to me, her eyes like a mirror reflecting my own image.

William Gerhardi

*L*ike one, like the other
Like daughter, like mother.

Anonymous

*C*hildren find comfort in flaws, ignorance, insecurities similar to their own. I love my mother for letting me see hers.

Erma Bombeck

*M*amas only do things 'cause they love you so much. They can't help it. It's flesh to flesh, blood to blood. No matter how old you get, how grown and on your own, your mama always loves you like a newborn.

Ntozake Shange

I think I'd be a good mother—
maybe a little overprotective. Like I would
never let the kid out—of my body!

Wendy Liebman

I get like a tigress when it's about my kids.

Meryl Streep

*W*hat tigress is there that
does not purr over her young ones, and fawn
upon them in tenderness?

Saint Augustine

• *182* •

*Y*outh fades; love droops; the leaves
of friendship fall:
A mother's secret love outlives them all.

Oliver Wendell Holmes

Dear Mom

*D*ear Mother: I'm all right.
Stop worrying about me.

Egyptian letter, 2000 B.C.

When God thought of Mother,
he must have laughed with satisfaction, and
framed it quickly—so rich, so deep, so
divine, so full of soul, power, and beauty,
was the conception.

Henry Ward Beecher

*O*h what a power is motherhood,
possessing a potent spell.

Euripides

I often think of my mother. Though I do not remember what she looked like, I feel her presence with me all the time. I still feel her warmth, her beauty. . . .

Eartha Kitt

$\mathcal{M}$y mother was the most
beautiful woman I ever saw. . . . All I am
I owe to my mother.

George Washington

*I*t was my mother who gave me my voice. She did this, I know now, by clearing a space where my words could fall, grow, then find their way to others.

Paula Giddings

*T*he shadow of my mother
danced around the room to a tune that my
shadow sang. . . .

Jamaica Kincaid

To describe my mother would be to write about a hurricane in its perfect power. Or the climbing, falling colors of a rainbow.

Maya Angelou

*I*t seems to me that my mother was the most splendid woman I ever knew.... If I have amounted to anything, it will be due to her.

Charles Chaplin

*M*y mother wanted me to be her wings, to fly as she never quite had the courage to do. I love her for that. I love the fact that she wanted to give birth to her own wings.

Erica Jong

A mother is not a person
to lean on but a person to make leaning
unnecessary.

Dorothy Canfield Fisher

*S*he's my teacher, my adviser,
my greatest inspiration.

Whitney Houston

*W*ho is it that loves me and will
   love me
forever with an affection which no
   chance,
no misery, no crime of mine can do
   away?—
It is you, my mother.

Thomas Carlyle

$\mathcal{M}$y mother was always someone who never laughed at my mistakes, who shared my pain and joys, who always stood beside me, never in front or behind me. She was as strong as an oak and yet as gentle as the morning dew, as beautiful as the sunset—and still is.

Ornetta Barber Dickerson

Mother, I love you so.
Said the child, I love you more than I
  know.
She laid her head on her mother's arm,
And the love between them kept them
  warm.

Stevie Smith

I am able to write about a good mother because I had a good mother—unequivocally. . . . She had a vested interest in making us feel good. At the time, I took it for granted that that's how mothers were, and now I just thank God almost every day.

Anna Quindlen

*L*et me not forget that I am the daughter of a woman . . . who herself never ceased to flower, untiringly, during three quarters of a century.

Colette

$\mathcal{I}$t doesn't matter how old I get,
whenever I see anything new or splendid, I
want to call, "Mom, come and look."

Helen Exley

$\mathcal{M}$ama! Dearest mama!
I know you are my one true friend.

Nikolai Gogol

*A*ll that I am or hope to be
I owe to my angel mother. I remember
my mother's prayers and they have always
followed me. They have clung to me all
my life.

Abraham Lincoln

*I*n the beginning there was my mother. A shape. A shape and a force, standing in the light. You could see her energy; it was visible in the air. Against any background she stood out.

Marilyn Krysl

My mother made a brilliant impression upon my childhood life. She shone for me like the evening star—I loved her dearly.

Winston Churchill

She knew how
to make virtues
out of necessities.

Audre Lorde

𝒴ou can choose your friends,
but you only have one mother.

Max Shulman

*M*other was one of those strong, restful, yet widely sympathetic natures, in whom all around seemed to find comfort and repose.

Harriet Beecher Stowe

$\mathcal{M}$y mother was as mild as any saint,
And nearly canonized by all she knew,
So gracious was her tact and tenderness.

Alfred, Lord Tennyson

I am all the time talking about you, and bragging, to one person or another. I am like the Ancient Mariner, who had a tale in his heart he must unfold to all. I am always buttonholing somebody and saying, "Someday you must meet my mother."

Edna St. Vincent Millay

$\mathcal{T}$he best advice from my
mother was a reminder to tell my children
every day: "Remember you are loved."

Evelyn McCormick

*H*undreds of stars in the pretty sky,
Hundreds of shells on the shore together,
Hundreds of birds that go singing by,
Hundreds of birds in the sunny weather,
Hundreds of dewdrops to greet the dawn,
Hundreds of bees in the purple clover,
Hundreds of butterflies on the lawn,
But only *one mother* the wide world over.

George Cooper

*M*y mother is a poem I'll never be able to write, though everything I write is a poem to my mother.

Sharon Doubiago

I cannot forget my mother. Though not as sturdy as others, she is my bridge. When I needed to get across, she steadied herself long enough for me to run across safely.

Renita Weems

$\mathcal{N}$ow that I am in my forties, she tells me I'm beautiful . . . and we have the long, personal and even remarkably honest phone calls I always wanted so intensely I forbade myself to imagine them. . . . With my poems, I finally won even my mother. The longest wooing of my life.

Marge Piercy

*L*enny always wanted an
audience. And in the beginning, I was his
audience.

Jennie Bernstein,
mother of Leonard Bernstein

*Y*ou too, my mother, read my
rhymes
For love of unforgotten times,
And you may chance to hear once more
The little feet along the floor.

Robert Louis Stevenson

$\mathcal{I}$'m never going to write my autobiography and it's all my mother's fault. I didn't hate her, so I have practically no material. In fact, the situation is worse than I'm pretending. We were crazy about her—and you know I'll never get a book out of that, much less a musical.

Jean Kerr

*I*n the heavens above,
The angels, whispering to one another,
Can find, among their burning terms of
   love,
None so devotional as that of "Mother."

Edgar Allan Poe

*W*here
else is love
that pure?
Susan Connors

God gives us friends—and that means
    much;
But far above all others,
The greatest of his gifts to Earth
Was when he thought of mothers.

Anonymous

Her
Gifts
to Us

$\mathcal{N}$ext to God we are indebted
to women, first for life itself, and then for
making it worth living.

Mary McLeod Bethune

For the mother is and must be, whether she knows it or not, the greatest, strongest, and most lasting teacher her children have.

Hannah Whitall Smith

*U*pon the mother devolves
the duty of planting in the hearts of her
children those seeds of love and virtue
which shall develop useful and happy lives.
There are no words to express the relation
of a mother to her children.

A. E. Davis

$\mathcal{A}$ mother has to give
her daughter her wings by giving her the
self-confidence to make decisions.

Priscilla Presley

$\mathcal{M}$y mother is a woman
who speaks with her life as much as with her
tongue.

Kesaya E. Noda

$\mathcal{M}$y mom's a survivor and
that's what she gave me. She's my only role
model.

Carrie Fisher

$\mathcal{M}$om is a tough friend.
I know she is going to be honest with me.

Robert Eldridge

*S*he tried in every way to understand me, and she succeeded. It was this deep, loving understanding as long as she lived that more than anything else helped and sustained me on my way to success.

Mae West

Mothers
always know.

Oprah Winfrey

*M*y mother is my root, my foundation. She planted the seed that I base my life on, and that is the belief that the ability to achieve starts in your mind.

Michael Jordan

$\mathcal{T}$he doctors told me I would
never walk, but my mother told me I would,
so I believed my mother.

Wilma Rudolph

Sometimes the strength of
motherhood is greater than natural laws.

Barbara Kingsolver

My mother's love for me
was so great that I have worked hard to
justify it.

Marc Chagall

I really learned it all from mothers.

Benjamin Spock

$\mathcal{M}$omma was home. She was the most totally human, human being that I have ever known; and so very beautiful. . . . Within our home, she was an abundance of love, discipline, fun, affection, strength, tenderness, encouragement, understanding, inspiration, support.

Leontyne Price

I thought my mom's whole
purpose was to be my mom. That's how she
made me feel.

Natasha Gregson Wagner

$\mathcal{M}$omma . . . rose alone
to apocalyptic silence, set the sun in our
windows, and daily mended the world.

Paulette Childress White

It's the three pairs of eyes that mothers have to have. . . . One pair that see through closed doors. Another in the back of her head . . . and, of course, the ones in front that can look at a child when he goofs up and reflect, "I understand and I love you," without so much as uttering a word.

Erma Bombeck

*M*y mother, who is my spiritual touchstone, told me to remember three things in life: "You have one body, respect it; one mind, feed it well; and one life— enjoy it."

Des'ree

And for the three magic gifts I needed to escape the poverty of my hometown, I thank my mother, who gave me a sewing machine, a typewriter, and a suitcase.

Alice Walker

I hear my mother when I'm being my best self—soothing someone else. . . . My mother's big message was that you take care of other people—whether it's the city of New Orleans, the Democratic party, or a little mutt from the pound.

Cokie Roberts

$\mathcal{M}$y mother had a slender, small body, but a large heart—a heart so large that everybody's grief and everybody's joy found welcome in it, and hospitable accommodation.

Mark Twain

$\mathcal{Y}$ou may have tangible wealth untold;
Caskets of jewels and coffers of gold.
Richer than I you can never be—
I had a mother who read to me.

Strickland Gillilan

$\mathcal{M}$y mother was not just
an interesting person, she was interested.

Joyce Maynard

*M*others, across cultures, are at the emotional center of the home and, collectively, of the world. They are channels of loving energy, the primary nurturers of all human beings. Mothers are quintessential people.

Alexandra Stoddard

It was my mother who taught
us to stand up to our problems, not only in
the world around us but in ourselves.

Dorothy   Pitman   Hughes

*M*ama exhorted her children at every opportunity to "jump at de sun." We might not land on the sun, but at least we would get off the ground.

Zora Neale Hurston

• 250 •

*M*y grandmothers were strong.
They followed plows and bent to toil.
They moved through fields sowing seeds.
They touched earth and grain grew.
They were full of sturdiness and singing.
My grandmothers were strong.
My grandmothers are full of memories. . . .

Margaret Walker

I still hear you humming, Mama. The color of your song calls me home. The color of your words saying, "Let her be. She got a right to be different. She gonna stumble on herself one of these days. Just let the child be." And I be, Mama.

Sonia Sanchez

$\mathcal{M}$y mother always told me how important dreams are. "Never give up on your dreams, because dreams are where reality begins," she said.

Marcia Y. Mahan

 *Y*ou must never feel that you
are less than anybody else. You must always
feel that you are somebody.

Alberta Williams King,
mother of Martin Luther King Jr.

I've always looked at the more positive side of things. All the pain I've had in my life, I'll hold on to it for a second and then I'll let it go. I really try to let go of all the negativity and leave the rest up to God. That's one of the beautiful gifts my mother gave me, the ability to allow certain things to be.

Diana Ross

$\mathcal{M}$y mother always said you can do whatever you want to. She always went after whatever she wanted and instilled that in me. She's very strong, very opinionated, never holds back.

Vanessa Williams

$\mathcal{I}$n the final analysis it is not what you do for your children but what you have taught them to do for themselves that will make them successful human beings.

Ann Landers

*W*hen I stopped seeing my
mother with the eyes of a child, I saw the
woman who helped me give birth to myself.

Nancy Friday

The precursor
of the mirror is
the mother's face.

D. W. Winnicott

She sacrificed to give us that
which she did not have when she was
growing up—leisure, emotional space, and
education.

Gloria Wade-Gayles

*Y*ou want to make the most
of every little scrap life gives you. My mother
taught me that.

Joyce Maynard

I owe my mother a great deal. She gave so unselfishly of herself and made many sacrifices for me. I hope she is proud of the person I have become.

Annette Jones White

My mother . . . taught me
many lessons:

Nothing is as it appears.

There are no calories in a broken cookie.

When in doubt, throw it out.

A stuffed animal is easier to care for than a
baby.

You can never own too many pairs of shoes.

Irene Zahava

*B*ecause of my mother it
never occurred to me that you couldn't do
what you wanted to do.

Francine Prose

The mother loves her child most divinely, not when she surrounds him with comfort and anticipates his wants, but when she resolutely holds him to the highest standards and is content with nothing less than his best.

Hamilton Wright Mabie

$\mathcal{I}$f it helps just one person,
it is worth doing." That's what Mama used
to say.

Sadie Delany

*E*verything I have learned about love,
I learned from my mother. . . . But mothers
absorb, accept, give in, all to tutor daughters
in the syntax, the grammar of yearning and
love.

Marita Golden

*S*he said that if I listened to her, later
I would know what she knew: where true
words came from, always from up high,
above everything else.

Amy Tan

$\mathcal{M}$y mother told me stories all the time. ...And in all of those stories she told me who I was, who I was supposed to be, whom I came from, and who would follow me. In this way, she taught me the meaning of the words she said, that all life is a circle and everything has a place within it.

Paula Gunn Allen

$\mathcal{M}$others . . . are the first
book read and the last put aside in every
child's library.

C. Lenox Remond

*T*o my first Love, my Mother,
   on whose knee
I learnt love-lore that is not troublesome.

Christina   Rossetti

The mother's heart is the child's schoolroom.

Henry Ward Beecher

*O*h, Mama was a smart woman.
It takes a smart woman to fall in love with a
good man.

Bessie Delany

What the mother sings
to the cradle goes all the way down to the
coffin.

Henry Ward Beecher

*M*ama always said, "Always
remember these words of wisdom which I
am about to impart to you, my dear. . . ."
and then she started snoring!

Dora J. Wilkenfeld

*W*ill you quit worrying about better ways to light the house and go get me some stove wood. You're not going to blow up the world this afternoon.

Nancy Elliot Edison,
mother of Thomas Alva Edison

*M*y mother was the source
from which I derived the guiding principles
of my life.

John Wesley

*I*t is the general rule, that all superior men inherit the elements of superiority from their mothers.

Michelet

I don't think Mama would have been at all surprised that Sadie and I have kept living this long. We learned a lot from her about being old. Mama set a good example.

Bessie Delany

*A*ll good traits and
learnings come from the mother's side.

Zora Neale Hurston

To Be a Mother

*S*uddenly she was here. And
I was no longer pregnant; I was a mother. I
never believed in miracles before.

Ellen Greene

*C*hildren
reinvent your
world for you.
Susan Sarandon

*M*aking the decision to have a child—it's momentous. It is to decide forever to have your heart go walking around outside your body.

Elizabeth Stone

Who takes the child by the
hand takes the mother by the heart.

Danish proverb

$\mathcal{M}$y daughter's birth was the incomparable gift of seeing the world at quite a different angle than before, and judging it by standards that would apply far beyond my natural life.

Alice Walker

$\mathcal{M}$otherhood is the greatest
thing that's ever happened to me.

Christie Brinkley

$\mathcal{I}$t is not until you become
a mother that your judgment slowly turns to
compassion and understanding.

Erma Bombeck

$\mathcal{M}$other's
love grows
by giving.

Charles Lamb

$\mathcal{I}$'ve gained a great feeling
of peace from being a mother. . . . The ability
to love is the heart of the matter.

Gloria Vanderbilt

I love being a mother. I am more aware. I feel things on a deeper level. I seem to have more of everything now: more love, more magic, more energy.

Shelley Long

There is a lot more to being a woman than being a mother. But there is a lot more to being a mother than most people suspect.

Roseanne

I must say that having children does really shed a different light on things. First of all, you have to stop putting yourself as number one, because you're not anymore. Somebody else is for a while.

Annie Lennox

I just couldn't live without children. . . . Motherhood has relaxed me in many ways. I've become a juggler, I suppose. It's all a big circus.

Jane Seymour

*L*ike so many things one did for children, it was absurd but pleasing, and the pleasure came from the anticipation of their pleasure.

Mary Gordon

I never thought that you
should be rewarded for the greatest privilege
of life.

Mary Roper Coker
1958 Mother of the Year

*Y*ou give up your self, and finally you don't even mind. I wouldn't have missed this for anything. It humbled my ego and stretched my soul. It gave me whatever crumbs of wisdom I possess today.

Erica Jong

$\mathcal{P}$arents learn a lot from
their children about coping with life.

Muriel Spark

$\mathcal{I}$ know how to do anything—
I'm a mom.

Roseanne

*P*eople see that you're no less effective because you're a mother. You become more focused and efficient with your time. You have to.

Gale Anne Hurd

$\mathcal{Y}$ou have a child, and you
can't be a perfectionist anymore.

Mary Beth Hurt

Let the men run around
trying to change the world. I just want to
improve my family.

Polly Judd,
mother of Naomi Judd

$\mathcal{E}$qual parenting" does not work—the maternal tuning in never turns off.

Phyllis Schlafly

*A*nyone who thinks mother
love is as soft and golden-eyed as a purring
cat should see a cat defending her kittens.

Pam Brown

*M*others have to tell themselves
that they mustn't feel guilty about anything.
We can't compare ourselves to the unattain-
able perfection of imaginary parents.

Tammy Grimes

$\mathcal{T}$hose parents are wise that
can fit their nurture according to their
Nature.

Anne Bradstreet

An atmosphere of trust, love, and humor can nourish extraordinary human capacity. One key is authenticity: parents acting as people, not as roles.

Marilyn Ferguson

*Y*ou never know in retrospect whether you did or didn't do exactly the right thing; stay-at-home mothers, gone-away mothers, all of us worry whether we should have done something differently than we did.

Hillary Rodham Clinton

• 308 •

$\mathcal{N}$o commitment in the whole world demands quite as much as bringing up children.

Janene Wolsey Baadsgaard

*B*eing a mother, as far as I can tell, is a constantly evolving process of adapting to the needs of your child while also changing and growing as a person in your own right.

Deborah Insel

*M*otherhood brings as much joy as ever, but it still brings boredom, exhaustion, and sorrow too. Nothing else will ever make you as happy or as sad, as proud or as tired, for nothing is quite as hard as helping a person develop his own individuality—especially while you struggle to keep your own.

*Marguerite Kelly
and Elia Parsons*

I do believe I am a good mother. I try to stay out of my children's way. I try to give them information because I worry, but you can't figure out all their problems for them. You can only assist.

Debbie Reynolds

*P*arents can only give good advice or put them on the right paths, but the final forming of a person's character lies in their own hands.

Anne Frank

$\mathcal{W}$hen a mother finally decides
to give her daughter some advice, the mother
usually learns plenty.

Evan Esar

*Y*ou can never really live anyone
else's life, not even your child's. The influence
you exert is through your own life, and
what you've become yourself.

Eleanor Roosevelt

I don't think there's any doubt that, for me, motherhood—and particularly my relationship with my daughter—has been one of the best experiences of my life. Watching someone grow and develop—someone who shares some of your views but not all of them, who struggles to find her own independent voice and her own identity—brings up a lot of the same issues that I face.

Hillary Rodham Clinton

*P*art of the good part of being a parent is a constant sense of *déjà vu*. But some of what you have to *vu* you never want to *vu* again.

Anna Quindlen

*M*y mother gave to me primarily by her example. She was willing to take risks, determined to provide us with opportunities she never had. And she did, as a woman, whatever she needed to do to be able to take care of herself and her children—by any means necessary.

Dr. Lenora Fulani

O, how little do children
know what parents sometimes endure for
their sake!

Mary Martha Sherwood

God knows a mother needs fortitude and
courage and tolerance and flexibility and patience
and firmness and nearly every other brave aspect
of the human soul. But . . . I praise casualness. It
seems to me the rarest of virtues. It's useful
enough when children are small. It is important to
the point of necessity when they are adolescents.

Phyllis McGinley

*I*n search of my
mother's garden
I found my own.
Alice Walker

*O*ver the years I have learned that motherhood is much like an austere religious order, the joining of which obligates one to relinquish all claims to personal possessions.

Nancy Stahl

*O*n one thing professionals
and amateurs agree: Mothers can't win.

Margaret Drabble

$\mathcal{T}$he joys of parents are secret,
and so are their griefs and fears.

Francis Bacon

*W*omen do not have to sacrifice personhood if they are mothers. They do not have to sacrifice motherhood in order to be persons.

Elaine Heffer

*H*ow are we to be the mothers
we want our daughters to have, if we are
still sorting out who our own mothers are
and what they mean to us?

Letty Cottin Pogrebin

I didn't realize how much I would learn from my children. They have shown me there are more important things than planning and organizing. They've given me more humanity.

Joanna Quillen

There is an amazed curiosity in every young mother. It is strangely miraculous to see and to hold a living being formed within oneself and issued forth from oneself.

Simone de Beauvoir

*Y*ou almost died," a nurse told her.
But that was nonsense. Of course she
wouldn't have died: She had children. When
you have children, you're obligated to live.

Anne Tyler

*C*hildren are the
anchors that hold
a mother to life.

Sophocles

I turn to look at my mother and she looks back at me. She knows my thoughts well, because they are very similar to her own. She has been thinking about the dreams I sometimes hear her dreaming.

Natasha Tarpley

*P*arenting, at its best, comes
as naturally as laughter. It is automatic,
involuntary, unconditional love.

Sally James

On
Motherhood

$\mathcal{G}$od could not be everywhere
and therefore made mothers.

Jewish proverb

*R*emember something always: I want you to live in the best place you can afford, eat well, and if there is anything left, send some to Mama.

Pearl Bailey

*K*ids have a way of bringing
purity back to life. That's what's important. To
raise children. Decent human beings.

Whitney Houston

*O*f all the rights of women,
the greatest is to be a mother.

Lin Yutang

*M*y first job
is to be a
good mother.

Faye Dunaway

*R*emember that your
child's character is like good soup. Both are
homemade.

Life's Little Instruction
Book, Vol. II

$\mathcal{T}$o say nothing of that brief but despotic sway which every woman possesses over the man in love with her—a power immense, unaccountable, invaluable; but in general so evanescent as but to make a brilliant episode in the tale of life—how almost immeasurable is the influence exercised by wives, sisters, friends, and, most of all, by mothers!

Anne Marsh

*T*he hand that rocks the
cradle is the hand that rules the world.

W. S. Ross

$\mathcal{I}$n God's great vaudeville, Mother is the headliner.

Elbert Hubbard

*S*pock, shlock, don't talk to me
about that stuff. A man doesn't know how to
bring up children until he's been a mother.

Dan   Greenburg

*I*f evolution really works,
how come mothers still have only
two hands?

Ed Dussault

*T*he hand that rocks the cradle
may not rule the world, but it certainly
makes it a better place.

Margery Hurst

To nourish children and raise them against odds is in any time, any place, more valuable than to fix bolts in cars or design nuclear weapons.

Marilyn French

A mother is a person who seeing there are only four pieces of pie for five people, promptly announces she never did care for pie.

Tenneva Jordan

We all like to live our lives again through our children. We know that we should do what is best for them. But unconsciously we do for them what we wish our parents had done for us.

Lee Kuan Yew

*W*e mothered this nation. And we have no intention of abandoning our roles as nurturer or wife, mother, loving daughter, tax-paying citizen, homemaker, breadwinner.

Liz Carpenter

I think we're seeing in working mothers a change from "Thank God It's Friday" to "Thank God It's Monday." If any working mother has not experienced that feeling, her children are not adolescent.

Ann Diehl

*L*ife does not begin at the moment of conception or the moment of birth. It begins when the kids leave home and the dog dies.

Anonymous

A mother is neither cocky, nor proud, because she knows the school principal may call at any minute to report that her child had just driven a motorcycle through the gymnasium.

Mary Kay Blakely

*I*f you must give your child lessons, send him to driving school. He is far more likely to end up owning a Datsun than he is a Stradivarius.

Fran Lebowitz

*I*f motherhood is an occupation which is critically important to society the way we say it is, then there should be a mother's bill of rights.

Barbara Ann Mikulski

$\mathcal{I}$t is still the biggest gamble in the world. It is the glorious life force. It's huge and scary—it's an act of infinite optimism.

Gilda Radner

Only mothers can think of
the future—because they give birth to it in
their children.

Maxim Gorky

*S*he broke the bread into two fragments and gave them to the children, who ate with avidity.

"She hath kept none for herself," grumbled the Sergeant.

"Because she is not hungry," said a soldier.

"Because she is a mother," said the Sergeant.

Victor Hugo

$\mathcal{W}$hat would I want
engraved on my gravestone for posterity?
"Mother."

Jessica Lange

A mother is not to be compared with another person—she is incomparable.

African proverb

A mother is she who can
take the place of all others but whose place
no one else can take.

Cardinal Mermillod

$\mathcal{M}$otherhood is the most
emotional experience of one's life. One joins
a kind of woman's mafia.

Janet Suzman

$\mathcal{B}$eing a mother makes me feel
as if I got my membership in an
exclusive club.

Andie MacDowell

I dig being a mother . . . and
of course, as a grandmother, I just
run amok.

Whoopi Goldberg

$\mathcal{H}$ousewives and mothers
seldom find it practicable to come out on
strike. They have no union, anyway.

Elaine Morgan

$\mathcal{P}$arenthood remains the
greatest single preserve of the amateur.

Alvin Toffler

The commonest fallacy among women is that simply having children makes one a mother—which is as absurd as believing that having a piano makes one a musician.

S. J. Harris

*W*omen who
miscalculate are
called mothers.

Abigail Van Buren

$\mathcal{R}$aising children is far
more creative than most jobs around for men
and women.

Benjamin Spock

*A*fter all, if you bungle
bringing up your children, it doesn't really
matter what you do with the rest of your life.

Sigourney Weaver

*I*t's not easy being a mother.
If it were, fathers would do it.

Dorothy
of The Golden Girls

$\mathcal{T}$he phrase "working mothers"
is redundant.

Jane Sellman

There are no ideal mothers, nor are there ideal daughters. Tension is intrinsic in the mother-daughter relationship and conflict is unavoidable.

Phyllis Magrab

*T*ogether, let's celebrate what it is
to be a mother. There is no more important
work than raising the next generation. This
is what mothers do.

Alexandra Stoddard

This book was
typeset in Bembo
and Piranesi by Nina Gaskin.

Book design by
Judith Stagnitto Abbate